THOMAS & FRIENDS™

SODOR'S LEGEND OF THE LOST TREASURE

EGMONT

We bring stories to life

First published in Great Britain 2015
by Egmont UK Limited
The Yellow Building
1 Nicholas Road
London W11 4AN

ISBN 978 1 4052 7759 4
60177/1
Printed in Great Britain

Chapter 1

It was a beautiful morning on the Island of Sodor. Thomas the Tank Engine was chuffing along his Branch Line with his coaches Annie and Clarabel.

"Faster! Faster!" puffed Thomas. "Bertie is just ahead. If I pass him, I'll win the race!"

"Slow down, Thomas!" cried Annie. "You know that The Fat Controller doesn't approve of racing."

Thomas wasn't listening. He just laughed and sped up, racing across the finish line just ahead of Bertie.

"Peep! Peep! I win!" Thomas cheered.

"That's not fair," said Bertie. "The roads are slower today because of the work on the new Branch Line."

Annie and Clarabel looked worried. "What if they close Thomas' Branch Line?" said Clarabel.

Thomas just smiled. "My Branch Line is the most important part of the whole Railway!" he said.

Meanwhile, at the new Branch Line construction site, everyone was very busy!

The workers were setting up dynamite to blast away the rocks and clear space for the new track.

"Stand back!" called the workers.

BOOM! RUMBLE! The ground shook.

"Everyone take care," said the Engineer. "We don't want anyone to fall through the cracks."

So the workers put up a safety barrier across the end of the track.

The next morning, Thomas couldn't get up. His fire kept going out and he didn't have enough steam.

"Wake up, lazybones," called Percy.

"That's what you get from too much racing," scolded Gordon.

Thomas was so sleepy he didn't even notice the red signal. He kept going and his coaches derailed!

The Fat Controller was not pleased. He sent Thomas to work on the new Branch Line. His newest tank engine, Ryan, would look after Thomas' Branch Line today.

Ryan was a very friendly engine. "Hello, Thomas!" he said.

But Thomas wasn't happy at all. He was worried The Fat Controller might close his Branch Line!

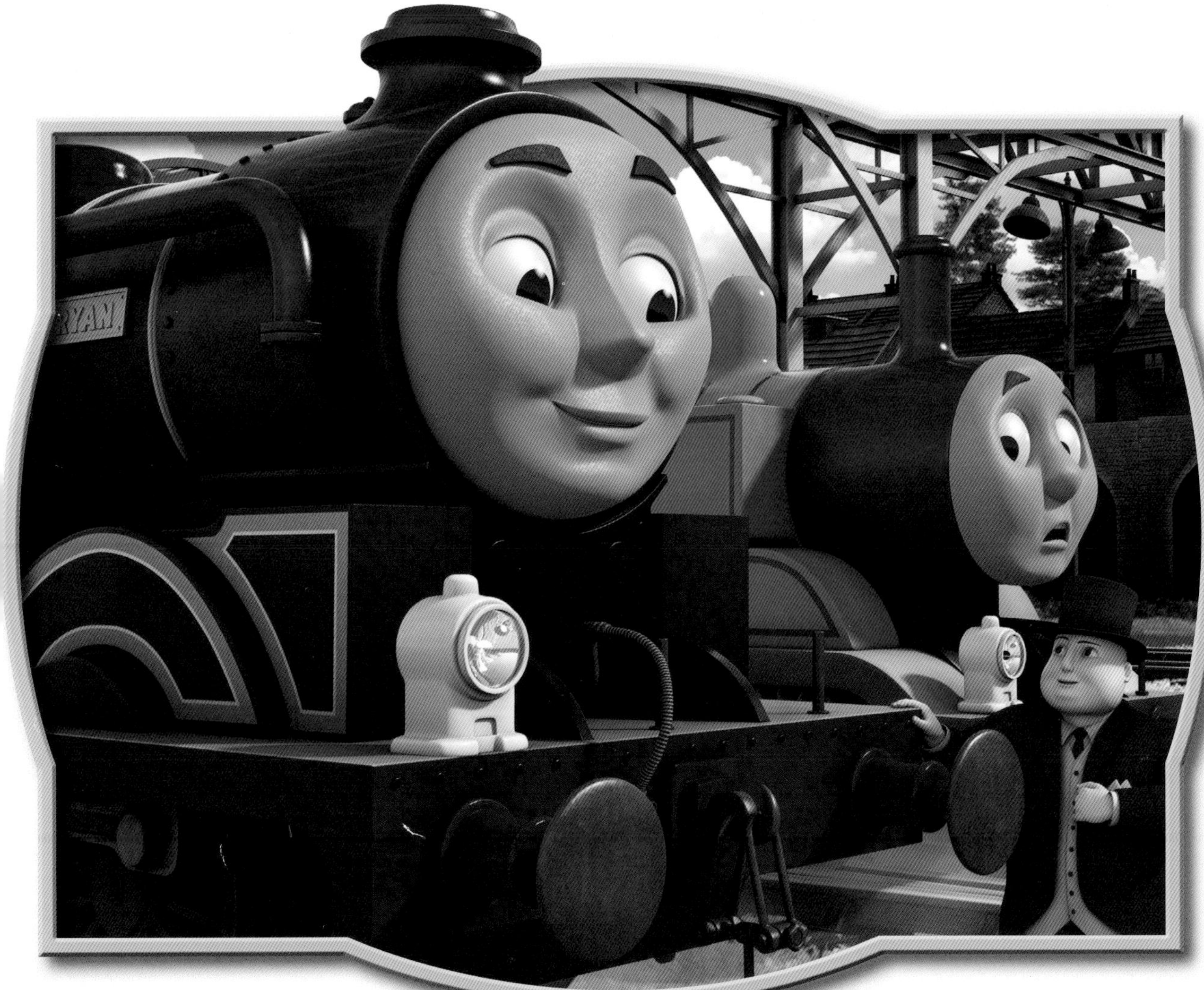

Thomas rushed off to the new Branch Line. He was in such a hurry, he didn't notice the danger signs!

"Stop, Thomas!" shouted the workers. But it was too late!

Thomas **crashed** through the barrier and tumbled down a giant hole in the ground.

"Cinders and ashes! What is this place?" Thomas cried.

He looked around. He was at the bottom of a dark cavern, next to something that looked like a giant ship!

Rocky the Breakdown Crane came to lift Thomas out.

The Fat Controller was waiting. "I'm very disappointed in you today, Thomas," he said.

Thomas tried to explain. "I didn't see the barrier, Sir! And I think there's something down in the cavern."

"I don't want to hear your excuses," The Fat Controller said sternly. "It's off to the Steamworks for you."

Now Thomas was **really** worried his Branch Line was going to be replaced!

Chapter 2

At the Steamworks, Victor and Kevin were repairing Thomas when Edward rushed up. "Rocky found an old pirate ship in the cavern!" he said excitedly.

"Rocky didn't find that ship.
I did!" Thomas said with a sigh.
But no one would listen.

Down at the Docks, Salty had a story to tell. "That pirate ship is probably The Lost Pirate Ship," he whispered. "Long ago, pirates were chased by the Navy. They hid in a cave on the Island of Sodor, but nobody ever found their lost treasure!"

The next morning, The Fat Controller sent Thomas back to the construction site. "I don't want any more trouble from you today," he said.

On his way, Thomas passed Rex, Bert and Mike, the Miniature Railway Engines. "It's not fair," Thomas complained. "I was the first to see the ship, not Rocky. And now I can't even work on my Branch Line."

"Cheer up," said Rex. "Look, there's Ryan shunting the dynamite for the new tracks."

But something was wrong. All the steam had caused the dynamite to spark.

"**Fizzling fireboxes!**" cried Thomas. "The dynamite could explode any minute!"

"**Help! Help!**" shouted Ryan.

Thomas had an idea. He chased after Ryan's burning trucks, and pushed them down into the cavern. The dynamite flew up into the air . . . and exploded!

BOOM!

Thomas sighed with relief. He was glad nobody was hurt!

"**THOMAS THE TANK ENGINE!**" bellowed The Fat Controller. "What are you playing at now?"

Thomas tried to explain that he had rescued Ryan, but The Fat Controller was too cross to listen. "I've had enough of you causing trouble," he said, frowning. "Go back to your Shed immediately."

Thomas chuffed back. By the time he passed the Harbour, he was feeling very sorry for himself.

Suddenly, he noticed a small boat bobbing up and down in the water.

"Hello," called Thomas.

"Well, blow me down! Who are you?" the sailor replied.

"I'm Thomas. I used to be The Fat Controller's Number One Engine . . . but I'm not anymore."

The sailor saluted. "My name's Sailor John. And this is my boat, Skiff. How would you like to help us search for pirate treasure tonight?"

Thomas couldn't wait to get started. Maybe if he could help find treasure, he could be a Really Useful Engine again!

Chapter 3

Late that night, Thomas crept out of his Shed and met Skiff and Sailor John down at the Harbour. Sailor John was holding a shovel and a lantern.

"We've been sailing up and down the coast for years searching for the pirates' lost treasure," Skiff told Thomas. "Sailor John built wheels for me, so I can roll on the tracks. I've always wanted to be a train, just like you!"

"**Shhh,**" whispered Sailor John. "Now show us where the pirate ship was found. Where there's a ship, there's treasure close by."

Thomas led the way to the cavern. Sailor John pulled out an old pirate map. "The treasure must be around here!" he said. But they searched all night and couldn't find it.

"We'll try again tomorrow night," Sailor John decided.

On his way home, Thomas bumped into Marion the Steam Shovel. "You look sad, Thomas," said Marion. "Do you know what always cheers me up? Digging!"

Clang! Marion's shovel hit something hard. It was a treasure chest! Marion was so surprised, she dropped it on Thomas.

"Bust my buffers!" Thomas said. "You found the buried treasure, Marion!"

The Fat Controller was very pleased. "Well done, Marion!" he said. "You are a Really Useful Steam Shovel."

Then The Fat Controller made plans for the treasure to go to the Sodor Museum, where everyone could see it.

At the new Branch Line, the engines couldn't stop talking about the buried treasure!

"Isn't this exciting, Thomas?" said Ryan. "I wanted to thank you for yesterday, too. You saved me from the burning dynamite. I'm sorry if I got you into trouble."

Everyone was very excited that the pirate treasure would be at the Sodor Museum . . . everyone, that is, except for Sailor John.

"How dare you find the treasure?" he sneered to Thomas. "I haven't been searching all this time for it to end up in a museum. It's for ME!"

Skiff looked sad. "You always said we were going to give it to a museum!" he said.

Sailor John stamped his foot. "This is not the end of it!" he scowled.

Chapter 4

Thomas couldn't stop worrying about whether the treasure would be safe. "I'll stay up all night so I can keep an eye on it," he said to himself.

Thomas found a place behind Knapford Station where he could keep watch. Soon, though, he began to feel sleepy. "I'll just close my eyes for a minute," he thought . . .

Zzzzz! Thomas fell fast asleep!

Not long after, Sailor John tiptoed past Thomas. He broke into The Fat Controller's office and stole all the treasure!

"Now it's all mine!" he sneered. "Time to go, Skiff!"

"Wait! This isn't right!" said Skiff, but it was too late! He was already rolling down the tracks back towards the Harbour.

The treasure chest was very heavy, and Skiff began to pick up speed. **"Whoaaa! Too fast!"** Skiff yelled.

Skiff's shouts awoke Thomas. "Oh, no!" he said. "They're getting away with the treasure!"

Thomas raced down the tracks after Sailor John. He couldn't catch up!

"You're too late, Thomas!" Sailor John smirked. "You can call me Pirate John now!"

Thomas sped up even more. “Stop that ship!” he called. “Come back with the treasure!”

Then Thomas reached the edge of the tracks. “Help!” cried Thomas. He was going so fast, he couldn’t stop!

SPLASH! Thomas toppled off the tracks and into the water.

"Goodbye, Thomas!" laughed Pirate John, paddling away. "Enjoy your swim!"

But the treasure chest was too heavy for Skiff. He began to wobble, back and forth.

"Hold fast, Skiff! Steady as she goes!" called Pirate John.

SPLASH! Skiff turned over, and Pirate John fell into the sea!

“**Noooo!**” cried Pirate John, as the pirate treasure disappeared beneath the waves.

Then Captain arrived with the police. “Hold it right there,” they called. The police pulled Pirate John out of the water, and placed him under arrest.

Thomas was rescued from the sea.

"I'm very proud of you, Thomas," said The Fat Controller. "You were very brave to try to stop that pirate getting away."

"But I wasn't quick enough to save the treasure, Sir," Thomas said sadly. "Now the lost treasure is lost again!"

The Fat Controller just smiled. "There are some things that are more important to me than any treasure. And you, Thomas, are my Number One Engine."

At last, Thomas was allowed to return to his Branch Line. The Fat Controller had another surprise for him as well. He had found better wheels for Skiff, so Skiff could run along the Branch Line, too!

"Peep! Peep!" cheered Thomas.

That afternoon, Captain carried divers out into the ocean.

SPLASH! SPLASH! The divers jumped into the water.

"They've found something!" called Captain. The divers had recovered the treasure chest. The lost pirate treasure could go on display at the Sodor Museum after all!

Later that day, everyone gathered at the new Branch Line.

“What will happen to my Branch Line?” Thomas asked The Fat Controller.

The Fat Controller chuckled. “Sodor needs you and your Branch Line, Thomas! This new Branch Line is for Ryan. You are both **Really Useful Engines!**”

The Fat Controller had a very special job for Thomas. "I'd like YOU to cut the ribbon for the new line," he said.

"Yes, Sir!" shouted Thomas. **"Full steam ahead!"**

"Three cheers for Thomas!" everyone called. And Thomas proudly led the parade of engines down the new Branch Line.

The End.